DISCARD

MR. MINTZ'S
BLINTZES

by Leslie Kimmelman

illustrated by Esther Hernando

APPLES & HONEY PRESS

To Clara and Stella,
who are both kind and delicious!
—LK

To my love and partner in life, and to
my mother and my grandmother
who I always remember, thank you
for your support and advice.
I love you.
—EH

Apples & Honey Press
An Imprint of Behrman House Publishers
Millburn, New Jersey 07041
www.applesandhoneypress.com

ISBN 978-1-68115-589-0

Text copyright © 2022 by Leslie Kimmelman
Illustrations copyright © 2022 by Behrman House

Library of Congress Cataloging-in-Publication Data

Names: Kimmelman, Leslie, author. | Hernando, Esther, illustrator.
Title: Mr. Mintz's blintzes / by Leslie Kimmelman ;
art by Esther Hernando.
Description: Millburn, New Jersey : Apples & Honey Press,
an imprint of Behrman House Publishers [2022] |
Audience: Ages 4-8. | Audience: Grades K-1. |
Summary: Mr. Mintz is the best of neighbors, and
everybody loves the blintzes he makes for his friends
for Shavuot, so when he is injured in an accident his
neighbors step in to take care of him and cook the
blintzes for him.
Identifiers: LCCN 2021042219 | ISBN 9781681155890 (hardcover)
Subjects: LCSH: Blintzes--Juvenile fiction. | Shavuot--Juvenile fiction. |
    Neighbors--Juvenile fiction. | Helping behavior--Juvenile fiction. |
    Conduct of life--Juvenile fiction. | CYAC: Blintzes--Fiction. |
    Shavuot--Fiction. | Neighbors--Fiction. | Helpfulness--Fiction. |
    Conduct of life--Fiction.
Classification: LCC PZ7.K56493 Mr 2022 | DDC 813.54 [E]--dc23
LC record available at https://lccn.loc.gov/2021042219

Design by Elynn Cohen
Edited by Aviva Lucas Gutnick and Ann D. Koffsky
Printed in the United States of America

9 8 7 6 5 4 3 2 1

MR. MINTZ was exactly the kind of neighbor everyone wanted.

He had a friendly word and a smile for everyone.

Plus, he was awesome at:

remembering birthdays,

raking leaves,

carrying groceries,

shoveling snow,

giving bike-riding lessons,

filling bird feeders,

and putting out
milk for the cats.

And oh, what a marvelous cook Mr. Mintz was!

He'd measure and mix and chop and pour. He'd add a spoonful of this and a pinch of that. He'd fill and fry and bake.

And in no time at all there'd be a dish of something so mouth-wateringly delicious that the aroma reached into every house on the street.

He gave away almost everything he made.

"What would I do with so much food?" Mr. Mintz said.

So he'd carry a pot of chicken soup to anyone who was feeling sick.

He'd offer latkes, sizzling hot, on Hanukkah.

And he'd deliver beautiful, braided loaves of challah on Friday afternoons, waving a cheery

"SHABBAT SHALOM!"

But best of all were Mr. Mintz's famous blintzes. He made them every spring for the holiday of Shavuot. They were absolutely scrumptious: cheesy and apple-y, sweet and savory, gooey and delicious.

"Shavuot celebrates the giving of the Torah to the Jewish people," thought Mr. Mintz. "It definitely deserves a bazillion blintzes."

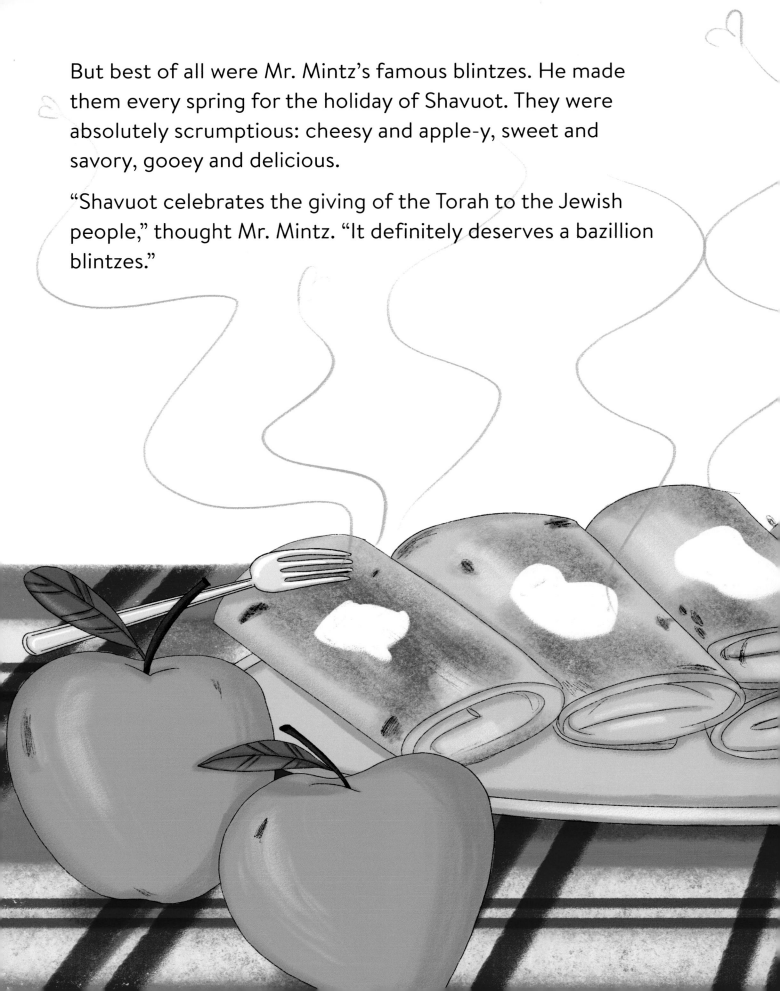

Then one year, just before Shavuot, something
TERRIBLE happened. Mr. Mintz was teaching
the twins next door a trick on his new skateboard.

"WATCH ME FLYYYY!"

he yelled excitedly.
He did not fly.

When Mr. Mintz
returned home the next
day, the house was dark and
still. "How will I manage?" he worried,
his voice echoing in the empty rooms.
Then he had another thought:

"I'm really hungry."

But it was a LONG,

LONG,

LONG

way to the kitchen.

Mr. Mintz heard the doorbell ring. "Come in!" he called. "Door's open!"

A parade of neighbors marched through. One neighbor helped him to the sofa and fluffed his pillows. Another brought him a cup of hot tea with honey. And a pair of purring kittens settled in his lap.

"You always take care of us," his neighbors told him.
"It's our turn to take care of you."

They measured and mixed and chopped and poured.
They added a spoonful of this and a pinch of that.
They filled and fried and baked.

And in no time at all, there was a gigantic mountain
of Mr. Mintz's (and friends') famous blintzes!

The wrappers were thin and delicate. The filling was cheesy and apple-y, sweet and savory, gooey and delicious. The aroma reached into every house on the street.

"Perfection!" said Mr. Mintz, helping himself to seconds.

Blintzes filled every stomach.

Happiness and kindness filled the room.

"This was the best Shavuot ever,"
proclaimed Mr. Mintz.
"With the best friends."

NOTE FROM THE AUTHOR

Shavuot celebrates the Jewish people receiving the Torah. Because the Torah is said to be nourishing, like milk, many people celebrate Shavuot by eating dairy foods such as cheese, ice cream, and blintzes.

Kindness is also worth celebrating. I grew up on a friendly street, much like Mr. Mintz's. My parents were always helping our neighbors with shoveling snow, gardening advice, and most of all, friendship. When a new neighbor moved in, my mother and father were the first to welcome them, usually with freshly baked cookies or cake—a tradition I have continued with my own family. (Blintzes work, too.)

Here's my blintz recipe. Try making a batch to share with your friends!

MR. MINTZ'S APPLE-CHEESE BLINTZES

(Be sure to have a grown up help you whenever using a sharp knife or stove!)

INGREDIENTS:

- 10 precooked crepes (available at most grocery stores)
- 1 pound ricotta cheese
- 4 tablespoons cream cheese
- 1 large egg yolk
- 1 tablespoon sugar
- ½ teaspoon grated lemon rind
- 1 large apple (or more, if desired), peeled and grated
- Dash cinnamon
- Butter

1. Make the filling: Mix together the ricotta cheese, cream cheese, egg yolk, sugar, and grated lemon rind. Refrigerate for at least 1 hour and up to 2 days.

2. Drain the filling through a sieve or piece of cheesecloth to remove excess liquid. Mix in grated apple and cinnamon.

3. Preheat over to 300 degrees F.

4. Spoon 3 tablespoons of filling in the middle of each crepe. Fold both sides into the middle, then fold the top down and the bottom up.

5. Melt 1 tablespoon butter in a heavy nonstick frying pan over medium-high heat. Working in batches, very carefully place blintzes in, seam sides down. Fry until lightly golden, then flip and fry on the other side. Be careful not to let the filling seep out. Place blintzes onto lined baking sheet or overproof baking dish. Repeat with rest of the blintzes.

6. Bake the blintzes for about 10 minutes, until heated through. Serve with sour cream or jam.